ReadZone Books Limited

50 Godfrey Avenue
Twickenham
TW2 7PF
UK

With thanks to Alex and Edward

© ReadZone Books 2014
© in text Su Swallow 2005
© in illustrations Silvia Raga 2005

Su Swallow has asserted her right under the Copyright Designs and Patents Act 1988
to be identified as the author of this work.

Silvia Raga has asserted her right under the Copyright Designs and Patents Act 1988
to be identified as the illustrator of this work.

First published in this edition by Evans Brothers Ltd, London in 2009.

Every attempt has been made by the Publisher to secure appropriate permissions for material
reproduced in this book. If there has been any oversight we will be happy to rectify the situation
in future editions or reprints. Written submissions should be made to the Publisher.

British Library Cataloguing in Publication Data (CIP) is available for this title.

Printed and bound in China for Imago

ISBN 978 1 78322 507 1

Visit our website: www.readzonebooks.com

The Sand Dragon

by Su Swallow

illustrated by Silvia Raga

Pale blue sky, deep blue sea, warm sand –
Edward raced along the beach,
happy to be at the seaside.

Splish splash, splish splash!
The boy bobbed along
with his boat

On the beach, Edward
searched for treasure.
He found shells –
thin ones and fat ones,
sharp ones and smooth
ones and shells like
wide slippery fans.

'This one is for you,' he said.

Hurrah! Castle complete.
Hard work, building a castle
out of sand.

Time for a rest.
Time to draw.

'What's that?' asked Mum,
as Edward drew in the sand.

'It's a sand dragon.'

'Say goodbye to sand dragon.
It's time to go home now.'

The sun went down.
The waves splashed on the shore.
The sand dragon lay on the beach.

As the tide rose, the sand dragon slipped into the water, and floated under the stars.

He dipped below the
waves and swam
among the seaweed,
nibbling the tasty fronds
as he explored the
watery world of the sea.

He danced and frolicked with the
sea creatures.

When it was time to go back, the sand dragon let the waves carry him back to shore.

The dragon lay on the sand to dry
and dream of his underwater adventures.

Edward came back, ready for
another day at the seaside.

What was that lying on the sand?
'Mummy, my sand dragon hasn't
moved all night!'